Sally Lumpkins' Party

A story of 6 true friends

Written by: Julianna Blankenship, Illustrated by: Deanna Dionne

To Emily Corie
Happy Reading!
Julianna
Blankenship

AuthorHouse™
1663 Liberty Drive, Suite 200
Bloomington, IN 47403
www.authorhouse.com
Phone: 1-800-839-8640

First published by AuthorHouse 1/22/2009

ISBN: 978-1-4343-6860-7 (sc)

Printed in the United States of America
Bloomington, Indiana

This book is printed on acid-free paper.

authorHOUSE®

For
millie

Sally Lumpkins was having a party,
and a grand one it would be.
Balloons and cakes and a pony ride,
candles and favors and me!

2

I was invited to SALLY'S PARTY.
THIS DAY, it WOULD be LiKE no other.

dress

doll

bear

I had bought her a bear
and a PiNK DRESS to wear
and a DOLL in need of a mother.

3

I wrapped up these gifts with the greatest of care
and a bow the size of Texas.
over, then cross, then around the loop,
I tied it tight and I fixed it.

4

I looked at the clock on our big wooden table.
The time seemed like it never would come.
I sat and I watched while that big yellow clock
ticked down the minutes 'til I would be able...

"Able for what?" your curious mind may ask,
"for what were you not able?"

I'll tell you, my friend, I waited on end
for that Dusty old clock on the table

to chime right at three, then time it would be
to round up my gifts and my wagon...

and head Down the street
to wave and to greet
my good friend, Allison Flagon.

ALLie was a gal of the prettiest of sorts
with hair the color of fire.

Her little pink nose
was scattered with rows
of freckles I had always admired.

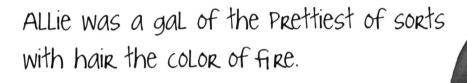

Allie

ALLie jumped down the stairs with her present in hand.
She looked like a leaf in her emerald green dress.

Not like a leaf on a tree,
she's more likely to be
a reed or a tall blade of grass!

7

Allie and I walked four houses down.
At this certain home there was never a frown.

For right now we stood
'front a house made of wood,
Painted pink as any in town!

In the blushing pink house on Mulberry Street
there lived a family of nine.
And friends with me, children 2 and 3,
were twins Ellie and Emma Valentine!

The twins burst through the door
with not a thought for
the ruckus they were leaving behind.

Their dark heads of curls
bobbed up, then unfurled
like spirals trying to unwind.

Emma

Ellie

I was back on the road
with three girls in tow
and a wagon filled with wrapped-up delights.

At last we arrived at Stockingwood Drive
to pick up our friend, Bekah Heights.

Bekah's long hair was flowing
and you had one way of knowing
when this girl had entered the room.

Her voice would travel
over mountain and gravel
and awaken you with a BOOM!

Bekah

Now five was our count,
an almost perfect amount-
Allie, Ellie, Emma, Bekah and me.

Now we would rally
and journey to Sally's.
Oh, what a grand day it would be!

Sally's house

SALLY lived in a big brick house
on the corner of Beech Street and Main.
Its tall stately steeples and statues of people
made it look like a castle in Spain.

speaking of spain, I cannot complain
of the streamers and ribbons and frills.

Sally's mother had sprung
for a silk table runner
and a vase with yellow daffodils

we curtsied and nodded
to our hostess who PRODDED us
over to the table for gifts.

I unloaded the wagon
and with all of the gifts gone
it looked like it needed a lift.

16

piñata

"It's time for the games!"
SALLY'S mother proclaimed
in a voice that commanded attention.

Pin a tail on a DONKEY,
and a Piñata monkey
with too much candy to mention.

17

But SALLY.....where was she?
At this Party so Lovely,
she was missing the fun and the games.

we all sat and PONDERED,
LOOKED 'ROUND 'bout and WONDERED
When SALLY WOULD come Down the Lane.

Sally

At the top of the stairs,
we stopped chatting and stared
at this picture of beauty so fair.

On top SALLY stood,
and stare we all would
at her RED DRESS
and Daisies in her hair.

We were so glad to see her, that Sally, standing up at the top of the stairs!

We ran up to greet her. The steps of our feet were echoing like an elephant pair!

Now six was our count, a perfect amount.
We had waited for this day to be.

Bekah and Sally,
Emma and Allie,
Ellie and last of all, me!

21

The party was great!
I ate so much cake that I felt like my sides might explode.

Ice cream with cherries
and chocolate strawberries
and a big cherry pie ala mode.

Now that clock that was always against me struck sad tones right at 6 o'clock.

I gathered my friends,
the party had ended,
now we had to head back down the block.

I don't like when parties are over,
It is such a sad time for all.
But never fear, we all live so near
all we do is make a telephone call!

The moral of this story,
in all of its glory,
is so simple anyone could tell.

Can you guess it now?
I'll tell you how
to explain it clear as a bell.

24

the Point of this tale
is that you never should fail
to appreciate friends while they're near.

for you never know when
the Party will end
and all will leave with a tear.

alli's house

Bekah's house

my house

Emma & Ellie's house

So, cherish family and friends
'til the very very end.
This truth you'll realize, I'm hoping.

For you never will find
any true peace of mind
'til your heart to them you open.

Sally's house

about the author...

Julianna Blankenship met all these wonderful friends at Rochester College in Rochester Hills, MI. She works in financial marketing and lives in Troy, MI, close to her crazy, fun family—Pat, Jim, Tiffany, Jimmy, Kaelyn, Arin, Scott, Zeke, Benjamin, Andrea, Bailey & Mulligan.

Sally Madurski Derrough aka "Sally Lumpkins"

Sally is a social worker living in Ann Arbor, MI. She is pursuing her social work masters at the University of Michigan & married to Joel.

Rebekah Parsons aka "Bekah Heights"

Rebekah calls Rochester, MI home, but currently lives in Arizona as a sports journalism graduate student at Arizona State University.

Allison Cox Milligan aka "Allison Flagon"

Allison is a financial administrator living in Rochester, MI. She is married to her college sweetheart, Sean.

Amy Jankowski Mitchell aka "Emma Valentine"

Amy is an executive non-profit administrator from Mt. Clemens, MI and married to Jeremy. If you're wondering about her character's name, spell "Emma" backwards.

Michelle Woody Lewis aka "Ellie Valentine"

Michelle hails from Indiana, New York, Michigan and, most recently, Arizona where she currently lives with her husband Ty & new baby Landon.

LaVergne, TN USA
10 March 2010
175547LV00002B